FAVOURITE

THOMAS THE TANK ENGINE STORIES

The Rev. W. Awdry

TREASURE PRESS

The story *Percy and the Trousers* is adapted from one told by
Mr C. Hamilton Ellis in *The Trains We Loved*. We gratefully
acknowledge his permission to use it.

The Railway Series by the Rev. W. Awdry is published by
William Heinemann Ltd,
an imprint of Reed International Books,
Michelin House, 81 Fulham Road, London SW3 6RB

LONDON MELBOURNE AUCKLAND

This edition published 1992 by Dean,
in association with Heinemann Young Books

ISBN 0 603 55089 4

Produced by Mandarin Offset
Printed in China.

CONTENTS

INTRODUCTION

In the filing cabinet in my study there is a large bundle of letters. They are all the letters which boys and girls, and grown-ups too, have sent me ever since the first of my little books was published. It always amazes me to think that when my son Christopher caught measles, and we made up our first story, we were starting a series of books which boys and girls would like so much.

It began quite simply. We had a little rhyme:

"Early in the morning, down at the station,
"All the little engines standing in a row.
"Along comes the driver, turns a little handle
"Puff, Puff, Chuff, Chuff, off we go."

"What was the engine's name, Daddy?" asked Christopher.

"Edward," I told him. It was the first name that came into my head.

"Why was he sad, Daddy?"

"Because he was old, and hadn't been out for a long time."

And so, with Christopher asking questions, and me thinking up answers, we made up the story which became the first story in the series about an engine called Edward.

I made Christopher a wooden push-along model of Edward and a wooden tank-engine which he called Thomas, and before long we had to have stories about Thomas the Tank Engine, too.

There are now thirty five books in the Railway Series, and boys and girls still like them even though no steam engines are left on British Rail, and you have to go to preserved lines like Bluebell, the Severn Valley, or the Talyllyn Railway to see them.

Many millions of Thomas the Tank Engine books have been sold, and in this special edition, several of the original Railway Series books appear together. I think this is a splendid idea. I hope you will like it.

GORDON
THE BIG ENGINE

Off the Rails

GORDON was resting in a siding. "Peep peep! Peep peep! Hullo, Fatface!" whistled Henry.

"What cheek!" spluttered Gordon. "That Henry is too big for his wheels; fancy speaking to me like that! Me e e e!" he went on, letting off steam, "Me e e e who has never had an accident!"

"Aren't jammed whistles and burst safety valves accidents?" asked Percy innocently.

"No indeed!" said Gordon huffily, "high spirits — might happen to any engine; but to come off the rails, well I ask you! Is it right? Is it decent?"

A few days later it was Henry's turn to take the Express. Gordon watched him getting ready.

"Be careful, Henry," he said, "you're not pulling the 'Flying Kipper' now; mind you keep on the rails today."

Henry snorted away, Gordon yawned and went to sleep.

But he didn't sleep long. "Wake up, Gordon," said his Driver, "a Special train's coming and we're to pull it."

Gordon opened his eyes. "Is it Coaches or Trucks?"

"Trucks," said his Driver.

"Trucks!" said Gordon crossly. "Pah!"

They lit Gordon's fire and oiled him ready for the run. The fire was sulky and wouldn't burn; but they couldn't wait, so Edward pushed him to the Turn-table to get him facing the right way.

"I won't go, I won't go," grumbled Gordon.

"Don't be silly, don't be silly," puffed Edward.

Gordon tried hard, but he couldn't stop himself being moved.

At last he was on the Turn-table, Edward was uncoupled and backed away, and Gordon's Driver and Fireman jumped down to turn him round.

The movement had shaken Gordon's fire; it was now burning nicely and making steam.

Gordon was cross, and didn't care what he did.

He waited till the Table was half-way round. "I'll show them! I'll show them!" he hissed, and moved slowly forward.

He only meant to go a little way, just far enough to "jam" the Table, and stop it turning, as he had done once before. But he couldn't stop himself, and, slithering down the embankment, he settled in a ditch.

"Oooosh!" he hissed as his wheels churned the mud. "Get me out! Get me out!"

"Not a hope," said his Driver and Fireman, "you're stuck, you silly great engine, don't you understand that?"

They telephoned the Fat Controller.

★　　★　　★

"So Gordon didn't want to take the Special and ran into a ditch," he answered from his office. "What's that you say? The Special's waiting – tell Edward to take it please – and Gordon? Oh leave him where he is; we haven't time to bother with him now."

A family of toads croaked crossly at Gordon as he lay in the mud. On the other side of the ditch some little boys were chattering.

"Coo! Doesn't he look silly!"

"They'll never get him out."

They began to sing:

> Silly old Gordon fell in a ditch,
>   fell in a ditch,
>   fell in a ditch,
> Silly old Gordon fell in a ditch,
> All on a Monday morning.

The School bell rang, and, still singing, they chased down the road.

"Pshaw!" said Gordon, and blew away three tadpoles and an inquisitive newt.

Gordon lay in the ditch all day.

"Oh dear!" he thought, "I shall never get out."

But that evening they brought floodlights; then with powerful jacks they lifted Gordon and made a road of sleepers under his wheels to keep him from the mud.

Strong wire ropes were fastened to his back end, and James and Henry, pulling hard, at last managed to bring him to the rails.

Late that night Gordon crawled home a sadder and a wiser engine!

Leaves

TWO MEN were cleaning Gordon.

"Mind my eye," Gordon grumbled.

"Shut it, silly! Did ever you see such mud, Bert?"

"No I never, Alf! You ought to be ashamed, Gordon, giving us extra work."

The hosing and scrubbing stopped. Gordon opened one eye, but shut it quickly.

"Wake up, Gordon," said the Fat Controller sternly, "and listen to me. You will pull no more coaches till you are a Really Useful Engine."

So Gordon had to spend his time pulling trucks.

"Goods trains, Goods trains," he muttered. He felt his position deeply.

"That's for you! – and *you*! – *and* you!" Gordon said crossly.

"Oh! Oh! Oh! Oh!" screamed the trucks as he shunted them about the yard.

"Trucks will be trucks," said James, watching him.

"They won't with *me*!" snorted Gordon. "I'll teach them. Go on!" and another truck scurried away.

"They tried to push me down the hill this morning," Gordon explained. "It's slippery there. You'll probably need some help."

"*I* don't need help on hills," said James huffily.

Gordon laughed, and got ready for his next train.

James went away to take the Express.

"Slippery hills indeed," he snorted. "*I* don't need help"

"Come on! Come on!" he puffed.

"All in good time, all in good time," grumbled the coaches.

The train was soon running nicely, but a "Distant" signal checked them close to Gordon's Hill.

Gordon's Hill used to be bleak and bare. Strong winds from the sea made it hard to climb. Trees were planted to give shelter, and

in summer the trains run through a leafy avenue.

Now Autumn had come, and dead leaves fell. The wind usually puffed them away, but today rain made them heavy, and they did not move.

The "Home" signal showed "clear", and James began to go faster.

He started to climb the hill.

"I'll do it! I'll do it!" he puffed confidently.

Half-way up he was not so sure! "I *must* do it, I *must* do it," he panted desperately, but try as he would, his wheels slipped on the leaves, and he couldn't pull the train at all.

"Whatsthematter? Whatsthematter?" he gasped. "Steady old boy, steady," soothed his Driver.

His Fireman put sand on the rails to help him grip; but James' wheels spun so fast that they only ground the sand and leaves to slippery mud, making things worse than before!

The train slowly stopped. Then –

"Help! Help! Help!" whistled James; for though his wheels were turning forwards, the heavy coaches pulled him backwards, and the whole train started slipping down the hill.

His Driver shut off steam, carefully put on the brakes, and skilfully stopped the train.

"Whew!" he sat down and mopped his face. "I've never known *that* happen before."

"I have," said the Fireman, "in Bincombe tunnel – Southern Region."

The Guard poked his head in the cab. "Now what?" he asked.

"Back to the station," said the Fireman, taking charge, "and send for a 'Banker'."

So the Guard warned the Signalman, and they brought the train safely down.

But Gordon, who had followed with a Goods train, saw what had happened.

Gordon left his trucks, and crossed over to James.

"I thought you could climb hills," he chuckled.

James didn't answer; he had no steam!

"Ah well! We live and learn," said Gordon, "we live and learn. Never mind, little James," he went on kindly, "I'm going to push behind. Whistle when you're ready."

James waited till he had plenty of steam, then "Peep! Peep!" he called.

"Poop! Poop! Poop!"

"Pull hard," puffed Gordon.

"We'll do it!" puffed James.

"Pull hard! We'll do it," the engines puffed together.

Clouds of smoke and steam towered from the snorting engines as they struggled up the hill.

"We *can* do it!" puffed James.

"We *will* do it!" puffed Gordon.

The greasy rails sometimes made Gordon's wheels slip, but he never gave up, and presently they reached the top.

"We've done it! We've done it!" they puffed.

Gordon stopped. "Poop! Poop!" he whistled. "Goodbye."

"Peep! Peep! Peep! Peep! Thank you! Goodbye," answered James. Gordon watched the coaches wistfully till they were out of sight; then slowly he trundled back to his waiting trucks.

Down the Mine

ONE DAY Thomas was at the junction, when Gordon shuffled in with some trucks.

"Poof!" remarked Thomas, "what a funny smell."

"Can you smell a smell?"

"I can't smell a smell," said Annie and Clarabel.

"A funny, musty sort of smell," said Thomas.

"No one noticed it till you did," grunted Gordon. "It must be yours."

"Annie! Clarabel! Do you know what I think it is?" whispered Thomas loudly. "It's ditchwater!"

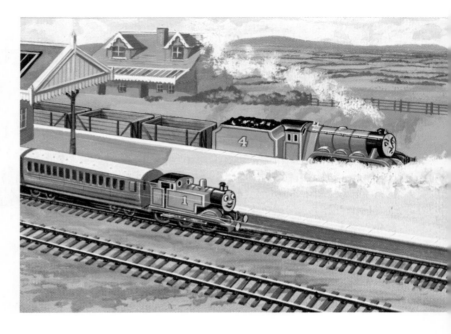

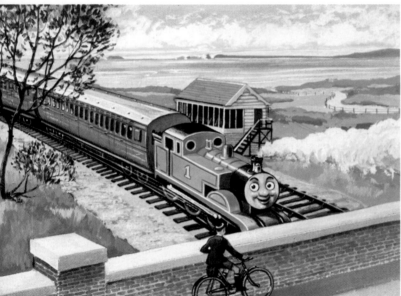

Gordon snorted, but before he could answer, Thomas puffed quickly away.

Annie and Clarabel could hardly believe their ears!

"He's *dreadfully* rude; I feel quite ashamed."

"I feel *quite* ashamed, he's dreadfully rude," they twittered to each other.

"You mustn't be rude, you make us ashamed," they kept telling Thomas.

But Thomas didn't care a bit.

"That was funny, that was funny," he chuckled. He felt very pleased with himself.

Annie and Clarabel were deeply shocked. They had a great respect for Gordon the Big Engine.

Thomas left the coaches at a station and went to a mine for some trucks.

Long ago, Miners, digging for lead, had made tunnels under the ground.

Though strong enough to hold up trucks, their roofs could not bear the weight of engines.

A large notice said: "DANGER. ENGINES MUST NOT PASS THIS BOARD."

Thomas had often been warned, but he didn't care.

"Silly old board," he thought. He had often tried to pass it, but had never succeeded.

This morning he laughed as he puffed along. He had made a plan.

He had to push empty trucks into one siding, and pull out full ones from another.

His Driver stopped him, and the Fireman went to turn the points.

"Come on," waved the Fireman, and they started.

The Driver leaned out of the cab to see where they were going.

"Now!" said Thomas to himself, and, bumping the trucks fiercely, he jerked his Driver off the footplate.

"Hurrah!" laughed Thomas, and he followed the trucks into the siding.

"Stupid old board!" said Thomas as he passed it.

"There's no danger; there's no danger."

His Driver, unhurt, jumped up . "Look out!" he shouted.

The Fireman clambered into the cab. Thomas squealed crossly as his brakes were applied.

"It's quite safe," he hissed.

"Come back," yelled the Driver, but before they could move, there was a rumbling and the rails quivered.

The Fireman jumped clear. As he did so the ballast slipped away and the rails sagged and broke.

"Fire and Smoke!" said Thomas, "I'm sunk!" – and he was!

Thomas could just see out of the hole, but he couldn't move.

"Oh dear!" he said, "I am a silly engine."

"And a very naughty one too," said a voice behind him, "I saw you."

"Please get me out; I won't be naughty again."

"I'm not so sure, "replied the Fat Controller. "We can't lift you out with a crane, the ground's not firm enough. H'm . . . Let me see . . . I wonder if Gordon could pull you out."

"Yes Sir," said Thomas nervously. He didn't want to meet Gordon just yet!

"Down a mine is he? Ho! Ho! Ho!" laughed Gordon.

"What a joke! What a joke!" he chortled, puffing to the rescue.

"Poop! Poop! little Thomas," he whistled, "we'll have you out in a couple of puffs."

Strong cables were fastened between the two engines.

"Poop! Poop! Poop! "

"Are you ready? HEAVE," called the Fat Controller.

But they didn't pull Thomas out in two puffs; Gordon was panting hard and nearly purple before he had dragged Thomas out of the hole, and safely past the board.

"I'm sorry I was cheeky," said Thomas.

"That's all right, Thomas. You made me laugh. I like that. I'm in disgrace," Gordon went on pathetically, "I feel very low"

"I'm in disgrace too," said Thomas.

"Why! so you are Thomas; we're both in disgrace.

Shall we form an Alliance?"

"An Ally – what – was – it?"

"An alliance, Thomas, 'United we stand, together we fall'," said Gordon grandly.

"You help me, and I help you. How about it?"

"Right you are," said Thomas.

"Good! That's settled," rumbled Gordon.

And buffer to buffer the Allies puffed home.

Paint Pots and Queens

THE STATIONS on the Line were being painted. The Engines were surprised.

"The Queen is coming," said the painters. The Engines in their shed were excited and wondered who would pull the Royal Train.

"I'm too old to pull important trains," said Edward sadly.

"I'm in disgrace," Gordon said gloomily. "The Fat Controller would never choose me."

"He'll choose me, of course," boasted James the Red Engine.

"You!" Henry snorted, "*You* can't climb hills. He will ask *me* to pull it, *and* I'll have a new coat of paint. You wait and see."

The days passed. Henry puffed about proudly, quite sure that he would be the Royal Engine.

One day when it rained, his Driver and Fireman stretched a tarpaulin from the cab to the tender to keep themselves dry.

Henry puffed into the big station. A painter was climbing a ladder above the line. Henry's smoke puffed upwards; it was thick and black. The painter choked and couldn't see. He missed his footing on the ladder, dropped his paint pot, and fell plop on to Henry's tarpaulin.

The paint poured over Henry's boiler, and trickled down each side. The paint pot perched on his dome.

The painter clambered down and shook his brush at Henry.

"You spoil my clean paint with your dirty smoke," he said, "and then you take the whole lot, and make me go and fetch some more." He stumped crossly away.

The Fat Controller pushed through the crowd.

"You look like an iced cake, Henry," he said. "*That* won't do for the Royal Train. I must make other arrangements."

He walked over to the Yard.

Gordon and Thomas saw him coming, and both began to speak.

"Please Sir – – – – – –."

"One at a time," smiled the Fat Controller. "Yes Gordon?"

"May Thomas have his Branch Line again?"

"Hm," said the Fat Controller, "well Thomas?"

"Please Sir, can Gordon pull coaches now?"

The Fat Controller pondered.

"Hm – – – – – – you've both been quite good lately, and you deserve a treat – – – – – When the Queen comes, Edward will go in front and clear the line, Thomas will look after the coaches, and Gordon – – – will pull the train."

"Ooooh Sir!" said the engines happily.

The great day came. Percy, Toby, Henry and James worked hard bringing people to the Town.

Thomas sorted all their coaches in the Yard.

"Peep! Peep! Peep! They're coming! "Edward steamed in, looking smart with flags and bright paint.

Two minutes passed – five – seven – ten. "Poop! Poop!" Everyone knew that whistle, and a mighty cheer went up as the Queen's train glided into the Station.

Gordon was spotless, and his brass shone. Like Edward, he was decorated with flags, but on his buffer he proudly carried the Royal Arms.

The Queen was met by the Fat Controller, and before doing anything else, she thanked him for their splendid run.

"Not at all, Your Majesty," he said, "thank *you*."

"We have read," said the Queen to the Fat Controller, "a great deal about your engines. May we see them please?"

So he led the way to where all the engines were waiting.

"Peep! Peep!" whistled Toby and Percy, "they're coming!"

"Sh Sh! Sh Sh!" hissed Henry and James.

But Toby and Percy were too excited to care.

The Fat Controller told the Queen their names and she talked to each engine. Then she turned to go.

Percy bubbled over, "Three cheers for the Queen!" he called.

"Peeeep! Peeeep! Peeeep!" whistled all the engines.

The Fat Controller held his ears, but the Queen, smiling, waved to the engines till she passed the gate.

The next day the Queen spoke specially to Thomas, who fetched her coaches, and to Edward and Gordon who took her away; and no engines ever felt prouder than Thomas, and Edward, and Gordon the Big Engine.

EDWARD
THE BLUE ENGINE

Cows!

EDWARD the blue engine was getting old. His bearings were worn, and he clanked as he puffed along. He was taking twenty empty cattle trucks to a market–town.

The sun shone, the birds sang, and some cows grazed in a field by the line.

"Come on! come on! come on!" puffed Edward.

"Oh! oh! oh! oh!" screamed the trucks.

Edward puffed and clanked; the trucks rattled and screamed. The cows were not used to trains; the noise and smoke disturbed them.

They twitched up their tails and ran.

They galloped across the field, broke through the fence, and charged the train between the thirteenth and fourteenth trucks. The coupling broke, and the last seven trucks left the rails. They were not damaged, and stayed upright. They ran for a short way along the sleepers before stopping.

Edward felt a jerk but didn't take much notice.

He was used to trucks.

"Bother those trucks!" he thought. "Why can't they come quietly?" He ran on to the next station before either he or his Driver realised what had happened.

When Gordon and Henry heard about the accident, they laughed and laughed. "Fancy allowing cows to break his train! They wouldn't dare do that to US. WE'd show them!" they boasted.

Edward pretended not to mind, but Toby was cross.

"You couldn't help it, Edward," he said. "They've never met cows. I have, and I know the trouble they are."

Some days later Gordon rushed through Edward's station.

"Poop poop!" he whistled, "mind the cows!"

"Haha, haha, haha!" he chortled, panting up the hill.

"Hurry, hurry, hurry!" puffed Gordon.

"Don't make such a fuss! Don't make such a fuss!" grumbled his coaches. They rumbled over the viaduct and roared through the next station.

A long straight stretch of line lay ahead. In the distance was a bridge. It had high parapets each side.

It seemed to Gordon that there was something on the bridge. His Driver thought so too. "Whoa, Gordon!" he said, and shut off steam.

"Pooh!" said Gordon, "it's only a cow!"

"SHOOH! SHOOH!" he hissed, moving slowly on to the bridge.

But the cow wouldn't "Shooh"! She had lost her calf, and felt lonely "Mooooh!" she said sadly, walking towards him.

Gordon stopped!

His Driver, Fireman and some Passengers tried to send her away, but she wouldn't go, so they gave it up.

Presently Henry arrived with a train from the other direction.

"What's this?" he said grandly. "A cow? I'll soon settle *her*. Be off! be off!" he hissed; but the cow turned and "moohed" at him. Henry backed away. "I don't want to hurt her," he said.

Drivers, Firemen and Passengers again tried to move the cow, but failed. Henry's Guard went back and put detonators on the line to protect his train. At the nearest station he told them about the cow.

"That must be Bluebell," said a Porter thoughtfully, "her calf is here, ready to go to market. We'll take it along. "

So they unloaded the calf and took it to the bridge.

"Mooh! mooh! "wailed the calf. "MOOH MOOH! "bellowed Bluebell.

She nuzzled her calf happily, and the Porter led them away.

The two trains started.

"Not a word."

"Keep it dark," whispered Gordon and Henry as they passed; but the story soon spread.

"Well, well, well!" chuckled Edward, "two big engines afraid of one cow!"

"Afraid – – Rubbish," said Gordon huffily. "We didn't want the poor thing to hurt herself by running against us. We stopped so as not to excite her. You see what I mean, my dear Edward."

"Yes, Gordon," said Edward gravely.

Gordon felt somehow that Edward "saw" only too well.

Bertie's Chase

"PEEP! peep! we're late," fussed Edward. "Peep! peep-pipeep! Where is Thomas? He doesn't usually make us wait."

"Oh dear, what can the matter be? . . ." sang the Fireman, "Johnnie's so long at . . ."

"Never you mind about Johnnie," laughed the Driver, "just you climb on the cab and look for Thomas." "Can you see him?"

"No."

The Guard looked at his watch. "Ten minutes late!" he said to the Driver, "we can't wait here all day."

"Look again, Sid," said the Driver, "just in case."

The Fireman got to his feet.

"Can you see him?"

"No," he answered, "there's Bertie 'bus in a tearing hurry. No need to bother with him though; likely he's on a Coach Tour or something." He clambered down.

"Right away, Charlie," said the Guard, and Edward puffed off.

"Toooot! TOOOT! Stop! STOP!" wailed Bertie roaring into the Yard, but it was no good. Edward's last coach had disappeared into the tunnel.

"Bother!" said Bertie. "Bother Thomas's Fireman not coming to work today. Oh why did I promise to help the Passengers catch the train?"

"That will do, Bertie," said his Driver, "a promise is a promise and we must keep it."

"I'll catch Edward or bust," said Bertie grimly, as he raced along the road.

"Oh my gears and axles!" he groaned, toiling up the hill. "I'll never be the same 'bus again!"

"Tootootoo Tootoot! I see him. Hurray! Hurray!" he cheered as he reached the top of the hill.

"He's reached the station," Bertie groaned the next minute.

"No . . . he's stopped by a signal. Hurray! Hurray!" and he tore down the hill, his brakes squealing at the corners.

His Passengers bounced like balls in a bucket. "Well done, Bertie," they shouted. "Go it! go it!"

Hens and dogs scattered in all directions as he raced through the village.

"Wait! wait!" he tooted, skidding into the Yard.

He was just in time to see the signal drop, the Guard wave his flag, and Edward puff out of the station.

His Passengers rushed to the platform, but it was no good, and they came bustling back.

"I'm sorry," said Bertie unhappily.

"Never mind, Bertie," they said. "After him quickly. Third time lucky you know!"

"Do you think we'll catch him at the next station, Driver?"

"There's a good chance," he answered. "Our road keeps close to the line, and we can climb hills better than Edward."

He thought for a minute. "I'll just make sure." He then spoke to the Stationmaster, while the Passengers waited impatiently in the 'bus.

"This hill is too steep! This hill is too steep!" grumbled the coaches as Edward snorted in front.

They reached the top at last and ran smoothly into the station.

"Peepeep!" whistled Edward, "get in quickly please."

The porters and people hurried and Edward impatiently waited to start.

"Peeeep!" whistled the Guard, and Edward's Driver looked back; but the flag didn't wave. There was a distant "Tooootoooot!" and the Stationmaster, running across, snatched the green flag out of the Guard's hand.

Then everything seemed to happen at once.

"Too too Toooooot!" bellowed Bertie; his Passengers poured on to the platform and scrambled into the train. The Stationmaster told the Guard and Driver what had happened, and Edward listened.

"I'm sorry about the chase, Bertie," he said.

"My fault," panted Bertie, "late at Junction . . . You didn't know . . . about Thomas's Passengers."

"Peepeep! Goodbye, Bertie, we're off!" whistled Edward.

"Three cheers for Bertie!" called the Passengers. They cheered and waved till they were out of sight.

Saved from Scrap

THERE is a scrap-yard near Edward's station. It is full of rusty old cars and machinery. They are brought there to be broken up. The pieces are loaded into trucks, and Edward pulls them to the Steelworks, where they are melted down and used again.

One day Edward saw a Traction–engine in the Yard.

"Hullo!" he said, "you're not broken and rusty. What are you doing there?"

"I'm Trevor," said the Traction–engine sadly, "they are going to break me up next week."

"What a shame!" said Edward.

"My Driver says I only need some paint, Brasso, and oil, to be as good as new," Trevor went on sadly, "but it's no good, my Master doesn't want me. I suppose it's because I'm old-fashioned."

Edward snorted indignantly, "People say *I'm* old-fashioned, but I don't care. The Fat Controller says I'm a Useful Engine."

"My Driver says I'm useful too," replied Trevor. "I sometimes feel ill, but I don't give up like these Tractors; I struggle on and finish the job. I've never broken down in my life," he ended proudly.

"What work did you do?" asked Edward kindly.

"My Master would send us from farm to farm. We threshed the corn, hauled logs, sawed timber, and did lots of other work. We made friends at all the farms, and saw them every year. The children loved to see us come. They followed us in crowds, and watched us all day long. My Driver would sometimes give them rides."

Trevor shut his eyes—remembering—

"I like children," he said simply. "Oh yes, I like children."

"Broken up, what a shame! Broken up, what a shame!" clanked Edward as he went back to work. "I *must* help Trevor, I *must*!"

He thought of the people he knew, who liked engines. Edward had lots of friends, but strangely none of them had room for a Traction engine at home!

"It's a shame! It's a shame!" he hissed as he brought his coaches to the station.

Then —

"Peep! peep!" he whistled, "why didn't I think of him before? "

Waiting there on the platform was the very person.

" 'Morning Charlie, 'Morning Sid. Hullo Edward, you look upset!"

"What's the matter, Charlie?" he asked the Driver.

"There's a Traction–engine in the scrap–yard, Vicar; he'll be broken up next week, and it's a shame. Jem Cole says he never drove a better engine."

"Do save him, Sir! You've got room, Sir!"

"Yes, Edward, I've got room," laughed the Vicar, "but I don't need a Traction-engine!"

"He'll saw wood, and give children rides. Do buy him, Sir, please!"

"We'll see," said the Vicar, and climbed into the train.

Jem Cole came on Saturday afternoon. "The Reverend's coming to see you, Trevor; maybe he'll buy you."

"Do you think he will?" asked Trevor hopefully.

"He will when I've lit your fire, and cleaned you up," said Jem.

When the Vicar and his two boys arrived in the evening, Trevor was blowing off steam. He hadn't felt so happy for months.

"Watch this, Reverence," called Jem, and Trevor chuffered happily about the Yard.

"Oh Daddy, do buy him," pleaded the boys, jumping up and down in their excitement.

"Now *I'll* try," and the Vicar climbed up beside Jem.

"Show your paces, Trevor," he said, and drove him into the Yard.

Then he went into the office, and came out smiling. "I've got him cheap, Jem, cheap."

"D'ye hear that, Trevor?" cried Jem. "The Reverend's saved you, and you'll live at the Vicarage now."

"Peep! Peep!" whistled Trevor happily.

"Will you drive him home for me, Jem, and take these scallywags with you? They won't want to come in the car when there's a Traction-engine to ride on!"

Trevor's home in the Vicarage Orchard is close to the railway, and he sees Edward every day. His paint is spotless and his brass shines like gold.

He saws firewood in winter, and Jem sometimes borrows him when a tractor fails. Trevor likes doing his old jobs, but his happiest day is the Church Fête. Then, with a long wooden seat bolted to his bunker, he chuffers round the Orchard giving rides to children.

Long afterwards you will see him shut his eyes – remembering –

"I like children," he whispers happily.

Old Iron

ONE day James had to wait at Edward's station till Edward and his train came in. This made him cross. "Late again!" he shouted.

Edward only laughed, and James fumed away.

"Edward is impossible," he grumbled to the others, "he clanks about like a lot of old iron, and he is so slow he makes us wait."

Thomas and Percy were indignant. "Old iron!" they snorted. "SLOW! Why! Edward could beat you in a race any day!"

"Really!" said James huffily, "I should like to see him do it.

One day James' Driver did not feel well when he came to work. "I'll manage," he said, but when they reached the top of Gordon's Hill, he could hardly stand.

The Fireman drove the train to the next station. He spoke to the Signalman, put the trucks in a siding, and uncoupled James ready for shunting.

Then he helped the Driver over to the station, and asked them to look after him, and find a "Relief".

Suddenly the Signalman shouted, and the Fireman turned round and saw James puffing away.

He ran hard but he couldn't catch James, and soon came back to the Signal-box. The Signalman was busy. "All traffic halted," he announced at last. "Up and down main lines are clear for thirty miles, and the Inspector's coming. "

The Fireman mopped his face. "What happened?" he asked.

"Two boys were on the footplate; they tumbled off when James started. I shouted at them and they ran like rabbits."

"Just let me catch them," said the Fireman grimly, "I'll teach them to meddle with my engine."

Both men jumped as the telephone rang; "Yes," answered the Signalman, "he's here . . . Right, I'll tell him.

"The Inspector's coming at once," said Edward. "He wants a shunter's pole, and a coil of wire rope."

"What for?" wondered the Fireman.

"Search me! But you'd better get them quickly."

The Fireman was ready and waiting when Edward arrived. The Inspector saw the pole and rope. "Good man," he said, "jump in."

"We'll catch him, we'll catch him," puffed Edward, crossing to the Up line in pursuit.

James was laughing as he left the Yard. "What a lark! what a lark!" he chuckled to himself.

Presently he missed his Driver's hand on the regulator . . . and then he realised there was no one in his cab . . . .

"What shall I do?" he wailed, "I can't stop. Help! Help!"

"We're coming, we're coming."

Edward was panting up behind with every ounce of steam he had. With a great effort, he caught up, and crept alongside, slowly gaining till his smokebox was level with James' buffer–beam.

"Steady, Edward."

The Inspector stood on Edward's front, holding a noose of rope in the crook of the shunter's pole. He was trying to slip it over James' buffer. The engines swayed and lurched. He tried again and again; more than once he nearly fell, but just saved himself.

At last – "Got him!" he shouted. He pulled the noose tight and came back to the cab safely.

Gently braking, so as not to snap the rope, Edward's Driver checked the engines' speed, and James' Fireman scrambled across and took control.

The engines puffed back side by side. "So the 'old iron' caught you after all!" chuckled Edward.

"I'm sorry," whispered James, "thank you for saving me"

"That's all right."

"You were splendid, Edward."

The Fat Controller was waiting, and thanking the men warmly. "A fine piece of work," he said. "James, you can rest, and then take your train. I'm proud of you, Edward; you shall go to the Works, and have your worn parts mended."

"Oh! Thank you, Sir!" said Edward happily. "It'll be *lovely* not to clank."

The two naughty boys were soon caught by the Police, and their Fathers walloped them soundly.

They were also forbidden to watch trains till they could be trusted.

James' Driver soon got well in hospital, and is now back at work. James missed him very much, but he missed Edward more, and you will be glad to know that, when Edward came home the other day, James and all the other engines gave him a tremendous welcome.

The Fat Controller thinks he will be deaf for weeks!

JAMES
THE RED ENGINE

James and the Top-Hat

JAMES was a new engine who lived at a station at the other end of the line. He had two small wheels in front and six driving wheels behind. They weren't as big as Gordon's, and they weren't as small as Thomas's.

"You're a special Mixed-Traffic engine," the Fat Controller told him. "You'll be able to pull coaches or trucks quite easily."

But trucks are not easy things to manage and on his first day they had pushed him down a hill into a field.

He had been ill after the accident, but now he had new brakes and a shining coat of red paint.

"The red paint will cheer you up after your accident," said the Fat Controller kindly. "You are to pull coaches today, and Edward shall help you."

They went together to find the coaches.

"Be careful with the coaches, James," said Edward, "they don't like being bumped. Trucks are silly and noisy; they need to be bumped and taught to behave, but coaches get cross and will pay you out."

They took the coaches to the platform and were both coupled on in front. The Fat Controller, the Station-Master, and some little boys all came to admire James's shining rods and red paint.

James was pleased. "I am a really splendid engine," he thought, and suddenly let off steam. "Whee-ee-ee-ee-eesh!"

The Fat Controller, the Station–Master and the guard all jumped, and a shower of water fell on the Fat Controller's nice new top–hat.

Just then the whistle blew and James thought they had better go – so they went!

"Go on, go on," he puffed to Edward.

"Don't push, don't push," puffed Edward, for he did not like starting quickly.

"Don't go so fast," grumbled the coaches; but James did not listen. He wanted to run away before the Fat Controller could call him back.

He didn't even want to stop at the first station. Edward tried hard to stop, but the two coaches in front were beyond the platform before they stopped, and they had to go back to let the passengers get out.

Lots of people came to look at James, and, as no one seemed to know about the Fat Controller's top–hat, James felt happier.

Presently they came to the junction where Thomas was waiting with his two coaches.

"Hullo, James!" said Thomas kindly, "feeling better? That's right. Ah! that's my guard's whistle. I must go. Sorry I can't stop. I don't know what the Fat Controller would do without me to run this branch line," and he puffed off importantly with his two coaches into a tunnel.

Leaving the junction, they passed the field where James had had his accident. The fence was mended and the cows were back again. James whistled, but they paid no attention.

They clattered through Edward's station-yard and started to climb the hill beyond.

"It's ever so steep, it's ever so steep," puffed James.

"I've done it before, I've done it before," puffed Edward .

"It's steep, but we'll do it – it's steep but we'll do it," the two engines puffed together as they pulled the train up the long hill.

They both rested at the next station; Edward told James how Gordon had stuck on the hill, and he had had to push him up!

James laughed so much that he got hiccoughs and surprised an old lady in a black bonnet.

She dropped all her parcels, and three porters, the Station–Master and the guard had to run after her picking them up!

James was quiet in the shed that night. He had enjoyed his day, but he was a little afraid of what the Fat Controller would say about the top–hat!

James and the Boot–lace

NEXT morning the Fat Controller spoke severely to James: "If you can't behave, I shall take away your red coat and have you painted blue."

James did not like that at all and he was very rough with the coaches as he brought them to the platform.

"Come along, come along," he called rudely.

"All in good time, all in good time," the coaches grumbled.

"Don't talk, come on!" answered James, and with the coaches squealing and grumbling after him, he snorted into the station.

James *was* cross that morning. The Fat Controller had spoken to him, the coaches had dawdled and, worst of all, he had had to fetch his own coaches.

"Gordon never does," thought James, "and he is only painted blue. A splendid Red Engine like me should never have to fetch his own coaches." And he puffed and snorted round to the front of the train, and backed on to it with a rude bump.

"O-ooooh!" groaned the coaches, "that was too bad!"

To make James even more cross, he then had to take the coaches to a different platform where no one came near him as he stood there. The Fat Controller was in his office, the Station-Master was at the other end of the train with the guard, and even the little boys stood a long way off.

James felt lonely. "I'll show them!" he said to himself. "They think Gordon is the only engine who can pull coaches. "

And as soon as the guard's whistle blew, he started off with a tremendous jerk.

"Come on! – come on! – come on!" he puffed, and the coaches, squeaking and groaning in protest, clattered over the points on to the open line.

"Hurry! – hurry – hurry!" puffed James.

"You're going too fast, you're going too fast," said the coaches, and indeed they were going so fast that they swayed from side to side.

James laughed and tried to go faster, but the coaches wouldn't let him.

"We're going to stop – we're going to stop – we're – going – to – stop," they said and James found himself going slower and slower.

"What's the matter?" James asked his driver.

"The brakes are hard on – leak in the pipe most likely. You've banged the coaches enough to make a leak in anything. "

The guard and the driver got down and looked at the brake pipes all along the train.

At last they found a hole where rough treatment had made a joint work loose.

"How shall we mend it?" said the guard.

James's driver thought for a moment.

"We'll do it with newspapers and a leather boot-lace."

"Well, where is the boot–lace coming from?" asked the guard . "We haven't one."

"Ask the passengers," said the driver.

So the guard made everyone get out.

"Has anybody got a leather boot–lace?" he asked.

They all said "No" except one man in a bowler hat (whose name was Jeremiah Jobling) who tried to hide his feet .

"You have a leather boot-lace there I see, sir," said the guard. "Please give it to me."

"I won't," said Jeremiah Jobling.

"Then," said the guard sternly, "I'm afraid this train will just stop where it is."

Then the passengers all told the guard, the driver and the fireman what a Bad Railway it was. But the guard climbed into his van, and the driver and fireman made James let off steam. So they all told Jeremiah Jobling he was a Bad Man instead.

At last he gave them his laces, the driver tied a pad of newspapers tightly round the hole, and James was able to pull the train.

But he was a sadder and a wiser James and took care never to bump coaches again.

Troublesome Trucks

JAMES did not see the Fat Controller for several days. They left James alone in the shed, and did not even allow him to go out and push coaches and trucks in the yard.

"Oh, dear!" he thought sadly, "I'll never be allowed out any more; I shall have to stay in this shed for always, and no one will ever see my red coat again. Oh, dear! Oh, dear!" James began to cry.

Just then the Fat Controller came along.

"I see you are sorry, James," he said. "I hope, now, that you will be a better Engine. You have given me a lot of trouble. People are laughing at my Railway, and I do not like that at all."

"I am very sorry, sir," said James. "I will try hard to behave. "

"That's a good engine," said the Fat Controller kindly. "I want you to pull some trucks for me. Run along and find them."

So James puffed happily away.

"Here are your trucks, James," said a little tank engine. "Have you got some boot–laces ready?" And he ran off laughing rudely.

"Oh! Oh! Oh!" said the trucks as James backed down on them. "We want a proper engine, not a Red Monster."

James took no notice and started as soon as the guard was ready.

"Come along, come along," he puffed.

"We won't! We won't!" screamed the trucks.

But James didn't care, and he pulled the screeching trucks sternly out of the yard.

The trucks tried hard to make him give up but he still kept on.

Sometimes their brakes would slip "on", and sometimes their axles would "run hot". Each time they would have to stop and put the trouble right, and each time James would start again, determined not to let the trucks beat him.

"Give up! give up! you can't pull us! You can't! You can't!" called the trucks.

"I can and I will! I can and I will!" puffed James.

And slowly but surely he pulled them along the line.

At last they saw Gordon's hill ahead.

"Look out for trouble, James," warned his driver.

We'll go fast and get them up before they know it. Don't let them stop you."

So James went faster, and they were soon halfway up the hill.

"I'm doing it! I'm doing it!" he panted.

But it was hard work.

"Will the top never come?" he thought, when with a sudden jerk it all came easier.

"I've done it! I've done it!" he puffed triumphantly.

"Hurrah!" he thought, "it's easy now." But his driver shut off steam.

"They've done it again," he said. "We've left our tail behind! "

The last ten trucks were running backwards down the hill. The coupling had snapped!

But the guard was brave. Very carefully and cleverly he made them stop. Then he got out and walked down the line with his red flag.

"That's why it was easy," said James as he backed the other trucks carefully down. "What silly things trucks are! There might have been an accident."

Meanwhile the guard had stopped Edward who was pulling three coaches.

"Shall I help you, James?" called Edward.

"No, thank you," answered James, "I'll pull them myself."

"Good, don't let them beat you."

So James got ready. Then with a "peep, peep" he was off.

"I *can* do it, I *can* do it," he puffed. He pulled and puffed as hard as he could.

"Peep pip peep peep! You're doing well!" whistled Edward, as James slowly struggled up the hill, with clouds of smoke and steam pouring from his funnel.

"I've done it, I've done it," he panted and disappeared over the top.

They reached their station safely. James was resting in the yard, when Edward puffed by with a cheerful "peep peep".

Then, walking towards him across the rails, James saw . . . the Fat Controller!

"Oh dear! what will he say?" he asked himself sadly.

But the Fat Controller was smiling. "I was in Edward's train, and saw everything," he said. "You've made the most troublesome trucks on the line behave. After that, you deserve to keep your red coat."

James and the Express

SOMETIMES Gordon and Henry slept in James's shed, and they would talk of nothing but boot-laces! James would talk about engines who got shut up in tunnels and stuck on hills, but they wouldn't listen, and went on talking and laughing.

"You talk too much, little James," Gordon would say. "A fine strong engine like me has something to talk about. I'm the only engine who can pull the Express. When I'm not there, they need two engines. Think of that!

"I've pulled expresses for years and have never once lost my way. I seem to know the right line by instinct," said Gordon proudly. Every wise engine knows, of course, that the signalman works the points to make engines run on the right lines, but Gordon was so proud that he had forgotten.

"Wake up, James," he said next morning, "it's nearly time for the Express. What are you doing? – Odd jobs? Ah well! We all have to begin somewhere, don't we? Run along now and get my coaches – don't be late now."

James went to get Gordon's coaches. They were now all shining with lovely new paint. He was careful not to bump them, and they followed him smoothly into the station singing happily. "We're going away, we're going away. "

"I wish I was going with you," said James. "I should love to pull the Express and go flying along the line."

He left them in the station and went back to the yard, just as Gordon with much noise and blowing of steam backed on to the train.

The Fat Controller was on the train with other Important People, and, as soon as they heard the guard's whistle, Gordon started.

"Look at me now! Look at me now!" he puffed, and the coaches glided after him out of the station.

"Poop poop poo poo poop! – Good-bye little James! See you tomorrow."

James watched the train disappear round a curve, and then went back to work. He pushed some trucks into their proper sidings and went to fetch the coaches for another train.

He brought the coaches to the platform and was just being uncoupled when he heard a mournful, quiet "Shush shush shush shush!" and there was Gordon trying to sidle into the station without being noticed.

"Hullo Gordon! Is it tomorrow?" asked James. Gordon didn't answer; he just let off steam feebly.

"Did you lose your way, Gordon?"

"No, it was lost for me," he answered crossly, "I was switched off the main line on to the loop; I had to go all round and back again."

"Perhaps it was instinct," said James brightly.

Meanwhile all the passengers hurried to the booking office. We want our money back," they shouted.

Everyone was making a noise, but the Fat Controller climbed on a trolley and blew the guard's whistle so loudly that they all stopped to look at him.

Then he promised them a new train at once.

"Gordon can't do it," he said. "Will you pull it for us, James?"

"Yes. sir, I'll try."

So James was coupled on and everyone got in again.

"Do your best, James," said the Fat Controller kindly. Just then the whistle blew and he had to run to get in.

"Come along, come along," puffed James.

"You're pulling us well! you're pulling us well," sang the coaches.

"Hurry, hurry, hurry," puffed James. Stations and bridges flashed by, the passengers leaned out of the windows and cheered, and they soon reached the terminus.

Everyone said "Thank you" to James. 'Well done," said the Fat Controller. "Would you like to pull the Express sometimes?"

"Yes, please," answered James happily.

Next day when James came by, Gordon was pushing trucks in the yard.

"I like some quiet work for a change," he said. "I'm teaching these trucks manners. You did well with those coaches I hear . . . good, we'll show them!" and he gave his trucks a bump, making them cry, "Oh!, Oh!, Oh!, Oh!"

James and Gordon are now good friends. James sometimes takes the Express to give Gordon a rest. Gordon never talks about bootlaces, and they are both quite agreed on the subjects of trucks!

HENRY
THE GREEN ENGINE

Coal

"I SUFFER dreadfully, and no one cares."

"Rubbish, Henry," snorted James, "you don't work hard enough."

Henry was bigger than James, but smaller than Gordon. Sometimes he could pull trains; sometimes he had no strength at all.

The Fat Controller spoke to him too. "You are too expensive, Henry. You have had lots of new parts and new paint too, but they've done you no good. If we can't make you better, we must get another engine instead of you."

This made Henry, his Driver, and his Fireman very sad.

The Fat Controller was waiting when Henry came to the platform. He had taken off his hat and coat, and put on overalls.

He climbed to the footplate and Henry started.

"Henry is a 'bad steamer'," said the Fireman. "I build up his fire, but it doesn't give enough heat."

Henry tried very hard, but it was no good. He had not enough steam, and they stopped outside Edward's station.

"Oh dear!" thought Henry sadly, "I shall have to go away."

Edward took charge of the train. Henry stopped behind.

"What do you think is wrong, Fireman?" asked the Fat Controller .

The Fireman mopped his face. "Excuse me, sir," he answered, "but the coal is wrong. We've had a poor lot lately, and today it's worse . The other engines can manage; they have big fireboxes. Henry's is small and can't make the heat. With Welsh coal he'd be a different engine."

"It's expensive," said the Fat Controller thoughtfully, "but Henry must have a fair chance. James shall go and fetch some."

When the Welsh coal came, Henry's Driver and Fireman were excited.

"Now we'll show them, Henry old fellow!" They carefully oiled all his joints and polished his brass till it shone like gold.

His fire had already been lit, so the Fireman "made it" carefully.

He put large lumps of coal like a wall round the outside. Then he covered the glowing middle part with smaller lumps.

"You're spoiling my fire," complained Henry.

"Wait and see," said the Fireman. "We'll have a roaring fire just when we want it."

He was right. When Henry reached the platform, the water was boiling nicely, and he had to let off steam to show how happy he was. He made such a noise that the Fat Controller came out to see him.

"How are you, Henry?"

"Pip peep peep!" whistled Henry, "I feel fine!"

"Have you a good fire, Driver?"

"Never better sir, *and* plenty of steam."

"No record breaking," warned the Fat Controller, smiling. "Don't push him too hard."

"Henry won't need pushing, sir; I'll have to hold him back."

Henry had a lovely day. He had never felt so well in his life. He wanted to go fast, but his Driver wouldn't let him. "Steady old fellow," he would say, "there's plenty of time."

They arrived early at the Junction.

"Where have you been, lazibones?" asked Henry, when Thomas puffed in, "I can't wait for dawdling Tank-Engines like you! Goodbye!"

"Whoooosh!" said Thomas to Annie and Clarabel as Henry disappeared, "have you ever seen anything like it?"

Both Annie and Clarabel agreed that they never had.

The Flying Kipper

Lots of ships use the harbour at the big station by the sea. The passenger ships have spotless paint and shining brass. Other ships, though smaller and dirtier, are important too. They take coal, machinery and other things abroad, and bring back meat, timber and things we need.

Fishing boats also come there. They unload their fish on the quay. Some of it is sent to shops in the town, and some goes in a special train to other places far away.

The railwaymen call this train "The Flying Kipper."

One winter evening Henry's Driver said: "We'll be out early tomorrow. We've got to take 'The Flying Kipper'."

"Don't tell Gordon," he whispered, "but I think if we pull the 'Kipper' nicely, the Fat Controller will let us pull the Express."

"Hurrah!" cried Henry, excited. "That will be lovely."

He was ready at 5 o'clock. There was snow and frost. Men hustled and shouted, loading the vans with crates of fish. The last door banged, the Guard showed his green lamp, and they were off.

"Come on! Come on! dontbesilly! – dontbesilly!" puffed Henry to the vans, as his wheels slipped on the icy rails .

The vans shuddered and groaned. "Trock, Trick, Trock, Trick; all right, all right," they answered grudgingly .

"That is better, that is better," puffed Henry more happily, as the train began to gather speed.

Thick clouds of smoke and steam poured from his funnel into the cold air; and when his Fireman put on more coal, the fire's light shone brightly on the snow around.

"Hurry, hurry, hurry," panted Henry.

They hooshed under bridges, and clattered through stations, green signal-lights showing as they passed.

They were going well, the light grew better and a yellow signal appeared ahead.

"Distant signal – up," thought Henry, "caution". His Driver, shutting off steam, prepared to stop, but the home signal was down. "All clear, Henry; away we go."

They couldn't know the points from the main line to a siding were frozen, and that that signal had been set at "danger". A fall of snow had forced it down.

A goods train waited in the siding to let "The Flying Kipper" pass. The Driver and Fireman were drinking cocoa in the brake-van.

The Guard pulled out his watch. "The Kipper' is due," he said.

"Who cares?" said the Fireman. "This is good cocoa."

The Driver got up, "Come on Fireman, back to our engine."

"Hey!" the Fireman grumbled, "I haven't finished my cocoa yet.

A sudden crash – the brake–van broke – the three men shot in the air like Jacks-in-the-box, and landed in the snow outside.

Henry's Driver and Fireman jumped clear before the crash. The Fireman fell head first into a heap of snow. He kicked so hard that the Driver couldn't pull him out.

Henry sprawled on his side. He looked surprised. The goods train Fireman waved his empty mug.

"You clumsy great engine! The best cup of cocoa I've ever had. and you bump into me and spill it all!"

"Never mind your cocoa, Fireman," laughed his Driver, run and telephone the breakdown gang."

The gang soon cleared the line, but they had hard work lifting Henry to the rails.

The Fat Controller came to see him.

"The signal was down, sir," said Henry nervously.

"Cheer up, Henry! It wasn't your fault. Ice and snow caused the accident. I'm sending you to Crewe, a fine place for sick engines. They'll give you a new shape and a larger firebox. Then you'll feel a different engine, and won't need special coal any more. Won't that be nice?"

"Yes, sir," said Henry doubtfully.

Henry liked being at Crewe, but was glad to come home.

A crowd of people waited to see him arrive in his new shape. He looked so splendid and strong that they gave him three cheers.

"Peep peep pippippeep! Thank you very much," he whistled happily.

I am sorry to say that a lot of little boys are often late for school because they wait to see Henry go by!

They often see him pulling the express; and he does it so well that Gordon is jealous. But that is another story.

Gordon's Whistle

GORDON was cross.

"Why should Henry have a new shape?" he grumbled. "A shape good enough for me is good enough for him. He goes gallivanting off to Crewe, leaving us to do his work. It's disgraceful!"

"And there's another thing. Henry whistles too much. No *respectable* engine ever whistles loudly at stations."

"It isn't wrong," said Gordon, "but we just don't do it."

Poor Henry didn't feel happy any more.

"Never mind," whispered Percy, "I'm glad you are home again; I like your whistling."

"Goodbye, Henry," called Gordon next morning as he left the shed. "We are glad to have you with us again, but be sure and remember what I said about whistling."

Later on Henry took a slow train, and presently stopped at Edward's station.

"Hullo Henry," said Edward, "you look splendid; I was pleased to hear your happy whistle yesterday."

"Thank you, Edward," smiled Henry . . . "Sh Sh! Can you hear something?"

Edward listened – far away, but getting louder and louder was the sound of an engine's whistle.

"It sounds like Gordon." said Edward, "and it ought to be Gordon, but Gordon never whistles like that."

It *was* Gordon.

He came rushing down the hill at a tremendous rate. He didn't look at Henry, and he didn't look at Edward; he was purple in the boiler, and whistling fit to burst.

He screamed through the station and disappeared.

"Well!!!" said Edward, looking at Henry.

"It isn't wrong," chuckled Henry, "but we just don't do it," and he told Edward what Gordon had said.

Meanwhile Gordon screeched along the line. People came out of their houses, air–raid sirens started, five fire brigades got ready to go out, horses upset their carts, and old ladies dropped their parcels.

At a big station the noise was awful. Porters and passengers held their ears. The Fat Controller held his ears too; he gave a lot of orders, but no one could hear them, and Gordon went on whistling. At last he clambered into Gordon's cab.

Take him away, he bellowed, "AND STOP THAT NOISE!"

Still whistling, Gordon puffed sadly away.

He whistled as he crossed the points; he whistled on the siding; he was still whistling as the last deafened passenger left the station.

Then two fitters climbed up and knocked his whistle valve into place –

– and there was SILENCE.

Gordon slunk into the shed. He was glad it was empty.

The others came in later. "It isn't wrong," murmured Henry to no one in particular, "but we just don't do it."

No one mentioned whistles!

Percy and the Trousers

ON COLD MORNINGS Percy often saw workmen wearing scarves.

"My funnel's cold, my funnel's cold!" he would puff; "I want a scarf, I want a scarf."

"Rubbish, Percy," said Henry one day, "engines don't want scarves!"

"Engines with proper funnels do," said Percy in his cheeky way. "You've only got a small one!"

Henry snorted; he was proud of his short, neat funnel.

Just then a train came in and Percy, still puffing "I want a scarf, I want a scarf," went to take the coaches to their siding.

His Driver always shut off steam just outside the station, and Percy would try to surprise the coaches by coming in as quietly as he could.

Two porters were taking some luggage across the line. They had a big load and were walking backwards, to see that none fell off the trolley.

Percy arrived so quietly that the porters didn't hear him till the trolley was on the line. The porters jumped clear. The trolley disappeared with a crunch.

Boxes and bags burst in all directions.

"Oo – oohe – r!" groaned Percy and stopped. Sticky streams of red and yellow jam trickled down his face. A top hat hung on his lamp–iron. Clothes, hats, boots, shoes, skirts and blouses stuck to his front. A pair of striped trousers coiled lovingly round his funnel. They were grey no longer!

Angry passengers looked at their broken trunks. The Fat Controller seized the top hat.

"Mine!" he said crossly.

"Percy," he shouted, "look at this."

"Yes sir, I am sir," a muffled voice replied.

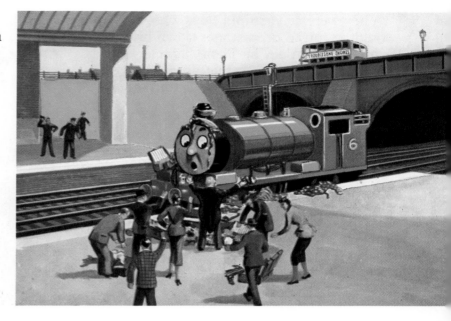

"My best trousers too!"

"Yes sir, please sir," said Percy nervously.

"I am very cross," said the Fat Controller. "We must pay the passengers for their spoilt clothes. My hat is dented, and my trousers are ruined, all because you will come into the station as if you were playing 'Grandmothers Steps' with the coaches."

The Driver unwound the trousers.

The Fat Controller waved them away.

"Percy wanted a scarf; he shall have my trousers for a scarf; they will keep him warm."

Percy wore them back to the yard.

He doesn't like scarves now!

Henry's Sneeze

ONE lovely Saturday morning, Henry was puffing along. The sun shone, the fields were green, the birds sang; Henry had plenty of steam in his boiler, and he was feeling happy.

"I feel so well, I feel so well," he sang.

"Trickety trock, Trickety trock," hummed his coaches.

Henry saw some boys on a bridge.

"Peep! Peep! Hullo!" he whistled cheerfully.

"Peep! Peep! Peeeep! "he called the next moment . "Oh! Oh! Oooh!" For the boys didn't wave and take his number; they dropped stones on him instead.

They were silly, stupid boys who thought it would be fun to drop stones down his funnel. Some of the stones hit Henry's boiler and spoilt his paint; one hit the Fireman on the head as he was shovelling coal, and others broke the carriage windows.

"It's a shame, it's a shame," hissed Henry.

"They've broken our glass, they've broken our glass," sobbed the coaches.

The Driver opened the first–aid box, bandaged the Fireman's head, and planned what he was going to do.

They stopped the train and the Guard asked if any passengers were hurt. No one was hurt but everyone was cross. They saw the Fireman's bumped head, and told him what to do for it, and they looked at Henry's paint. "Call the Police," they shouted angrily.

"No!" said the Driver, "leave it to Henry and me. We'll teach those lads a lesson."

"What will you do?" they asked. "Can you keep a secret?" "Yes, yes," they all said. "Well then," said the Driver, "Henry is going to sneeze at them."

"What!" cried all the passengers.

The Driver laughed. "Henry draws air in through his fire, and puffs it out with smoke and steam. When he puffs hard, the air blows ashes from his fire into his smoke box, and these ashes sometimes prevent him puffing properly.

"When your nose is blocked, you sometimes sneeze. If Henry's smoke box is blocked, I can make air and steam blow the ashes out through his funnel.

"We will do it at the bridge and startle those boys."

Henry puffed on to the terminus, where he had a rest. Then he took the train back. Lots of people were waiting at the station just before the bridge. They wanted to see what would happen.

"Henry has plenty of ashes," said the Driver. "Please keep all windows shut till we have passed the bridge. Henry is as excited as we are, aren't you old fellow?" and he patted Henry's boiler.

Henry didn't answer; he was feeling "stuffed up", but he winked at his Driver, like this.

The Guard's flag waved, his whistle blew, and they were off. Soon in the distance they saw the bridge. There were the boys, and they all had stones.

"Are you ready, Henry?" said his Driver. "Sneeze hard when I tell you."

"Now!" he said, and turned the handle.

"Atisha Atisha Atishooooooh!"

Smoke and steam and ashes spouted from his funnel. They went all over the bridge, and all over the boys who ran away as black as soot.

"Well done, Henry," laughed his Driver, "they won't drop stones on engines again."

"Your coat is all black, but we'll rub you down and paint your scratches and you'll be as good as new tomorrow.

Henry has never again sneezed under a bridge. The Fat Controller doesn't like it. His smoke box is always cleaned in the yard while he is resting.

He has now gone under more bridges than he can count; but from that day to this there have been no more boys with stones.

THE
THREE RAILWAY ENGINES

Edward's Day Out

ONCE upon a time there was a little engine called Edward. He lived in a shed with five other engines. They were all bigger than Edward and boasted about it.

"The driver won't choose you again," they said. "He wants big, strong engines like us."

Edward had not been out for a long time;

he began to feel sad. Just then the driver and fireman came along to start work.

The driver looked at Edward. "Why are you sad?" he asked. "Would you like to come out today?"

"Yes, please," said Edward. So the fireman lit the fire and made a nice lot of steam.

Then the driver pulled the lever, and Edward puffed away.

"Peep, peep," he whistled. "Look at me now."

The others were very cross at being left behind.

Away went Edward to get some coaches.

"Be careful, Edward," said the coaches, "don't bump and bang us like the other engines do." So Edward came up to the coaches, very, very gently, and the shunter fastened the coupling.

"Thank you, Edward," said the coaches. "That was kind, we are glad you are taking us today."

Then they went to the station where the people were waiting.

"Peep, peep," whistled Edward – "get in quickly, please."

So the people got in quickly and Edward waited happily for the guard to blow his whistle, and wave his green flag.

He waited and waited – there was no whistle, no green flag. "Peep, peep, peep, peep – where is that guard?" Edward was getting anxious.

The driver and fireman asked the Stationmaster, "Have you seen the guard?" "No," he said. They asked the porter, "Have you seen the guard?" "Yes – last night," said the porter.

Edward began to get cross. "Are we ever going to start?" he said.

Just then a little boy shouted, "Here he comes!" and there the guard was, running down the hill with his flags in one hand and a sandwich in the other.

He ran on to the platform, blew his whistle, and jumped into his van.

Edward puffed off. He did have a happy day. All the children ran to wave as he went past and he met old friends at all the stations. He worked so hard that the driver promised to take him out again next day.

"I'm going out again tomorrow, "he told the other engines that night in the shed. "What do you think of that? "

But he didn't hear what they thought, for he was so tired and happy that he fell asleep at once.

Edward and Gordon

One of the engines in Edward's shed was called Gordon. He was very big and very proud.

"You watch me this afternoon, little Edward," he boasted, "as I rush through with the express; that will be a splendid sight for you."

Just then his driver pulled the lever. "Goodbye, little Edward," said Gordon, as he puffed away, "look out for me this afternoon!"

Edward went off, too, to do some shunting.

Edward liked shunting. It was fun playing with trucks. He would come up quietly and give them a pull.

"Oh! Oh! Oh! Oh! Oh!" screamed the trucks. "Whatever is happening?"

Then he would stop and the silly trucks would go bump into each other. "Oh! Oh! Oh! Oh!" they cried again.

Edward pushed them until they were running nicely, and when they weren't expecting it he would stop; one of them would be sure to run on to another line.

Edward played till there were no more trucks; then he stopped to rest.

Presently he heard a whistle. Gordon came puffing along, very slowly, and very crossly. Instead of nice shining coaches, he was pulling a lot of very dirty coal trucks.

"A goods train! a goods train! a goods train!" he grumbled. "The shame of it, the shame of it."

He went slowly through, with the trucks clattering and banging behind him.

Edward laughed, and went to find some more trucks.

Soon afterwards a porter came and spoke to his driver. "Gordon can't get up the hill. will you take Edward and push him, please?"

They found Gordon halfway up the hill and very cross. His driver and fireman were talking to him severely. "You are not trying!" they told him.

"I can't do it," said Gordon. "The noisy trucks hold an engine back so. If they were coaches now – clean sensible things that come quietly – that would be different."

Edward's driver came up. "We've come to push," he said. "No use at all," said Gordon. "You wait and see," said Edward's driver.

They brought the train back to the bottom of the hill. Edward came up behind the brake van ready to push.

"Peep, peep, I'm ready," said Edward.

"Poop, poop, no good," grumbled Gordon.

The guard blew his whistle and they pulled and pushed as hard as they could.

"I can't do it, I can't do it, I can't do it," puffed Gordon.

"I will do it, I will do it, I will do it," puffed Edward.

"I can't do it, I will do it, I can't do it, I will do it, I can't do it, I will do it," they puffed together.

Edward pushed and puffed and puffed and pushed, as hard as ever he could, and almost before he realized it, Gordon found himself at the top of the hill.

"I've done it! I've done it! I've done it!" he said proudly, and forgot all about Edward pushing behind. He didn't wait to say "Thank you", but ran on so fast that he passed two stations before his driver could make him stop .

Edward had pushed so hard that when he got to the top he was out of breath.

Gordon ran on so fast that Edward was left behind.

The guard waved and waved, but Edward couldn't catch up.

He ran on to the next station, and there the driver and fireman said they were very pleased with him. The fireman gave him a nice long drink of water, and the driver said, "I'll get out my paint tomorrow, and give you a beautiful new coat of blue with red stripes, then you'll be the smartest engine in the shed."

The Sad Story of Henry

ONCE, an engine attached to a train
Was afraid of a few drops of rain –

– It went into a tunnel,
And squeaked through its funnel
And never came out again.

The engine's name was Henry. His driver
and fireman argued with him, but he would
not move. "The rain will spoil my lovely
green paint and red stripes," he said.

The guard blew his whistle till he had no
more breath, and waved his flags till his arms
ached; but Henry still staved in the tunnel,
and blew steam at him.

"I am not going to spoil my lovely green
paint and red stripes for you," he said rudely.

The passengers came and argued too, but Henry would not move.

A fat director who was on the train told the guard to get a rope. "We will pull you out," he said. But Henry only blew steam at him and made him wet.

They hooked the rope on and all pulled – except the fat director. "My doctor has forbidden me to pull," he said.

They pulled and pulled and pulled, but still Henry stayed in the tunnel.

Then they tried pushing from the other end. The fat director said, "One, two, three, push": but did not help. "My doctor has forbidden me to push," he said.

They pushed and pushed and pushed; but still Henry stayed in the tunnel.

At last another train came. The guard waved his red flag and stopped it. The two engine drivers, the two firemen, and the two

guards went and argued with Henry. "Look, it has stopped raining," they said. "Yes, but it will begin again soon," said Henry. "And what would become of my green paint with red stripes then?"

So they brought the other engine up, and it pushed and puffed and pushed as hard as ever it could. But still Henry stayed in the tunnel.

So they gave it up. They told Henry, "We shall leave you there for always and always and always."

They took up the old rails, built a wall in front of him, and cut a new tunnel.

Now Henry can't get out, and he watches the trains rushing through the new tunnel. He is very sad because no one will ever see his lovely green paint with red stripes again.

But I think he deserved it, don't you?

Edward, Gordon and Henry

EDWARD and Gordon often went through the tunnel where Henry was shut up.

Edward would say, "Peep, peep – hullo!" and Gordon would say, "Poop, poop, poop! Serves you right!"

Poor Henry had no steam to answer, his fire had gone out; soot and dirt from the tunnel roof had spoilt his lovely green paint and red stripes. He was cold and unhappy, and wanted to come out and pull trains too.

Gordon always pulled the express. He was proud of being the only engine strong enough to do it.

There were many heavy coaches, full of important people like the fat director who had punished Henry.

Gordon was seeing how fast he could go. "Hurry! hurry! hurry!" he panted.

"Trickety–trock, trickety–trock, trickety–trock," said the coaches.

Gordon could see Henry's tunnel in front.

"In a minute," he thought, "I'll poop, poop, poop at Henry, and rush through and out into the open again."

Closer and closer he came – he was almost there, when crack: Wheee————eeshshsh," he was in a cloud of steam, and going slower and slower.

His driver stopped the train.

"What has happened to me?" asked Gordon, "I feel so weak." "You've burst your safety valve," said the driver. "You can't pull the train any more." "Oh dear," said Gordon. "We were going so nicely, too. . . . Look at Henry laughing at me." Gordon made a face at Henry, and blew smoke at him.

Everybody got out, and came to see Gordon. "Humph!" said the fat director. "I never liked these big engines – always going wrong; send for another engine at once."

While the guard went to find one, they uncoupled Gordon and ran him on a siding out of the way.

The only engine left in the shed was Edward.

"I'll come and try," he said.

Gordon saw him coming. "That's no use," he said, "Edward can't pull the train."

Edward puffed and pulled, and pulled and puffed, but he couldn't move the heavy coaches.

"I told you so," said Gordon rudely. "Why not let Henry try?"

"Yes," said the fat director, "I will."

"Will you help pull this train, Henry?" he asked. "Yes," said Henry at once.

So Gordon's driver and fireman lit his fire; some platelayers broke down the wall and put back the rails; and when he had steam up Henry puffed out.

He was dirty, his boiler was black, and he was covered with cobwebs. "Ooh! I'm so stiff! Ooh! I'm so stiff!" he groaned.

"You'd better have a run to ease your joints and find a turntable," said the fat director kindly.

Henry came back feeling better, and they put him in front.

"Peep, peep," said Edward, "I'm ready"

"Peep, peep, peep," said Henry, "so am I."

"Pull hard; pull hard; pull hard," puffed Edward.

"We'll do it; we'll do it; we'll do it," puffed Henry.

"Pull hard we'll do it. Pull hard we'll do it. Pull hard we'll do it," they puffed together. The heavy coaches jerked and began to move, slowly at first, then faster and faster.

"We've done it together! We've done it together! We've done it together!" said Edward and Henry.

"You've done it, hurray! You've done it, hurray! You've done it, hurray!" said the coaches.

All the passengers were excited. The fat director leaned out of the window to wave to Edward and Henry; but the train was going so fast that his hat blew off into a field where a goat ate it for his tea.

They never stopped till they came to the big station at the end of the line.

The passengers all got out and said, "Thank you", and the fat director promised Henry a new coat of paint.

"Would you like blue and red?"

"Yes, please," said Henry, "then I'll be like Edward."

Edward and Henry went home quietly, and on their way they helped Gordon back to the shed.

All three engines are now great friends.

Wasn't Henry pleased when he had his new coat. He is very proud of it, as all good engines are – but he doesn't mind the rain now, because he knows that the best way to keep his paint nice is not to run into tunnels, but to ask his driver to rub him down when the day's work is over.

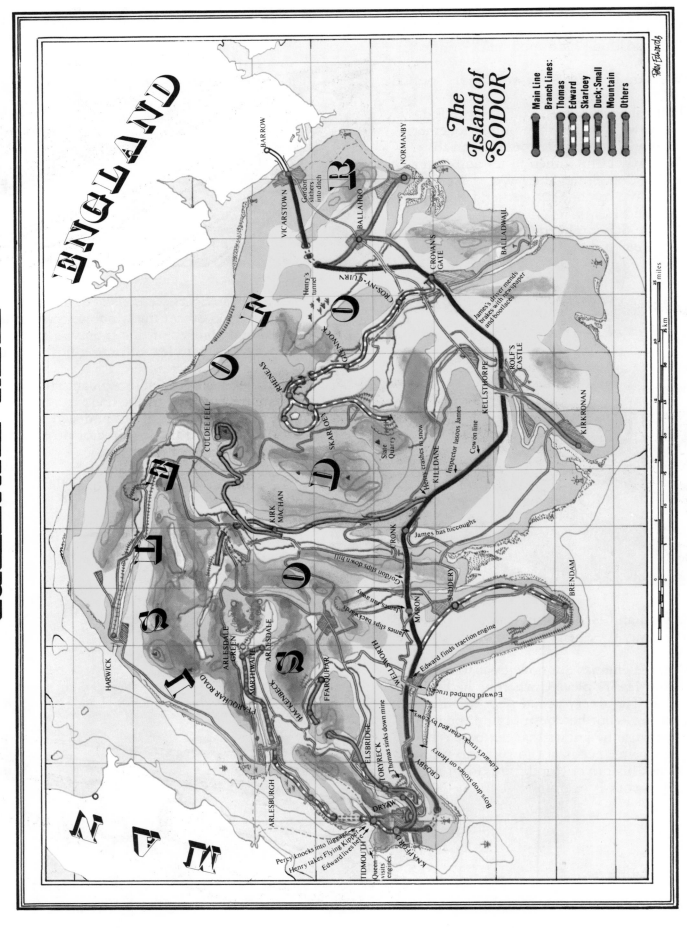

RAILWAY MAP

ENGLAND

MAN

The Island of SODOR

Main Line
Branch Lines:
Thomas
Edward
Skarloey
Duck; Small
Mountain
Others

BARROW

VICARSTOWN

Gordon slithers into ditch

Henry's tunnel

BALLAHOO

CROVAN'S GATE

CROS-NY-CUIRN

James's driver mends brakes with newspaper and bootlaces

NORMANBY

BALLADWAIL

ROLF'S CASTLE

KELLSTHORPE

KIRKRONAN

RHENEAS

SKARLOEY

Slate Quarry

Henry crashes in snow

KILLDANE

Inspector lassos James

Cow on line

CULDEE FELL

KIRK MACHAN

CRONK

James has hiccoughs

SUDDERY

Gordon slips down hill

James runs away

James slips backwards

MARON

BRENDAM

Edward finds traction engine

WELLSWORTH

Edward bumped truck

Edward's trucks charged by cows

Boys drop stones on Henry

HARWICK

FFARQUHAR ROAD

ARLESDALE GREEN

MARTHWAITE

ARLESDALE

HACKENBECK

FFARQUHAR

ELSBRIDGE

Thomas sinks down mine

TORYRECK

CROSBY

DRYAW

ARLESBURGH

KNAPFORD

TIDMOUTH

Percy knocks into luggage

Henry takes Flying Kipper

Edward lives here

Queen visits engines

miles

km